Bad Nature

The New Directions Pearls

Federico García Lorca, *In Search of Duende*

Javier Marías, *Bad Nature, or With Elvis in Mexico*

Yukio Mishima, *Patriotism*

Tennessee Williams, *Tales of Desire*

Forthcoming

César Aira, *The Literary Conference*

Jorge Luis Borges, *Everything & Nothing*

Bad Nature
or With Elvis in Mexico

•

JAVIER MARÍAS

Translated by Esther Allen

A NEW DIRECTIONS PEARL

First published in Spain in 1996 as *Mala Indole*

Published by arrangement with Mercedes Casanovas Agencia Literaria, Barcelona

Bad Nature first appeared in English in *Granta* in 1999.

Manufactured in the United States of America
New Directions Books are printed on acid-free paper.
First published as a Pearl (NDP1165) by New Directions in 2010
Published simultaneously in Canada by Penguin Books Canada Limited
Design by Erik Rieselbach

Library of Congress Cataloging-in-Publication Data

Marías, Javier.
[Mala indole. English] Bad nature, or With Elvis in Mexico / by Javier
Marías ; translated by Esther Allen.
p. cm.
"A New Directions Pearl."
ISBN 978-0-8112-1858-0 (pbk. : acid-free paper)
1. Presley, Elvis, 1935-1977—Fiction. I. Allen, Esther, 1962– II. Title.
PQ6663.A7218M3513 2009
863'.64—dc22   2009039623

10 9 8 7 6 5 4 3 2 1

New Directions Books are published for James Laughlin
by New Directions Publishing Corporation
80 Eighth Avenue, New York, NY 10011

For someone who's laughing in my ear

NO ONE KNOWS what it is to be hunted down without having lived it, and unless the chase was active and constant, carried out with deliberation, determination, dedication and never a break, with perseverance and fanaticism, as if the pursuers had nothing else to do in life but look for you, keep after you, follow your trail, locate you, catch up with you and then, at best, wait for the moment to settle the score. It isn't that someone has it in for you and stands at the ready to pounce should you cross his path or give him the chance; it isn't that someone has sworn revenge and waits, waits, does no more than wait and therefore remains passive, or schemes in preparation for his blows, which as long as they're machinations cannot be blows, we think the blows will fall but they may not, the enemy may drop dead of a heart attack before he sets to work in earnest, before he truly applies himself to harming us, destroying us. Or he may forget, calm down, something may distract him and he may forget, and if we don't happen to cross his path again we may be able to get away; vengeance is extremely wearying and hatred tends to evaporate, it's a fragile, ephemeral feeling, impermanent, fleeting, so difficult to maintain that it quickly gives way to rancor or

1

resentment which are more bearable, easier to retrieve, much less virulent and somehow less pressing, while hatred is always in a tearing hurry, always urgent: I want him now, I want him dead, bring me the son of a bitch's head, I want to see him flayed and his body smeared with tar and feathers, a carcass, skinned and butchered, and then he will be no one and this hatred that is exhausting me will end.

No, it isn't that someone would harm you if given the chance, it isn't one of those civilized enmities in which someone takes a certain satisfaction in striking a name off the list of invitees to the embassy ball, or publishes nothing in his section of the newspaper about his rival's achievements, or fails to invite to a conference the man who once took a job away from him. It isn't the betrayed husband who does his utmost to pay back the betrayal —or do what he thinks will pay it back—and see you betrayed in turn, it isn't even the man who trusted you with his savings and was had, buying in advance a house that was never built or going up to his eyeballs in debt to finance a film when there was never the slightest intention of shooting a single millimeter of footage, it's incredible how the movies lure and delude people. Nor is it the writer or painter who didn't win the prize that went to you, and believes his life would have been different if only justice had been done back then, twenty years ago; it isn't even the peon thrashed a thousand times by the vicious and abusive capataz who is the owner's right-hand man, the peon who yearns for a new Zapata in whose wake he'll slip a knife all the way down his tor-turer's belly and, in passing, across the landowner's jugular, because the peon, too, lives in a state of waiting, or rather of that childish daydreaming we all fall into from time to time in order to make ourselves remember our desires, that is, in order to keep from forgetting them, and though repetition would appear to be in the service of memory, in fact it blurs and plays tricks on memory and mutes it, relegating our needs to the sphere of that which is to come, so that nothing seems to de-pend on us right now, nothing depends on the peon, and the capataz knows there is a vague or imaginary threat and suffers from his own dream, a dream of fear that makes him the more brutal and vicious, repaying in ad-vance the knife thrust to the belly that he receives only in dreams, his own and those of others.

No, being hunted down is none of those things; it isn't knowing that you could be hunted down, it isn't know-ing who would come to kill you if another civil war were to break out in these countries of ours, so prone to war, so full of rage, it isn't knowing with absolute certainty that someone would stamp on your hand if it were clutching the edge of a cliff (a thing we don't usually risk, not in the presence of heartless people), it isn't fearing a bad encounter that could be avoided by walking down other streets or going to other bars or visiting other houses, it isn't worrying that fate will make a mockery of us or the tables will be turned against us one day, it isn't making possible or probable enemies or even certain but always future ones, committing transgressions whose atonement lies far ahead, almost everything is put off, almost nothing is immediate or exists in the present, and we live in a state of postponement, life usually consists only of delay, of signs and plans, of projects and machinations, we trust in the indolence and infinite lethargy of the whole world, the indolence of knowing that things will come about and come to pass, and the indolence of carrying them out.

But sometimes there is neither indolence nor lethargy nor childish daydreaming, sometimes — though rarely — there is the urgency of hatred, the negation of reprieve and cunning and stratagems, which are present only if improvised by the intolerable resistance of the one being pursued and exist merely as setbacks, without other power than to cause a slight adjustment to the planned trajectory of a bullet because the target has moved and evaded it. This time. But never again, or that's the hope; if the bullet went astray, the only thing to do is fire again, and again and again until the mark falls and can be finished off. When you're being hunted down like that you feel as if your pursuers do nothing but search for you, chase you twenty-four hours a day: you're convinced that they don't eat or sleep, they don't drink or stop even for one second, their venomous footsteps are incessant and tireless and there is no rest; they have neither wife nor child nor needs, they don't need to pee, they don't pause to chat, they don't get laid or go to soccer games, they don't have television sets or homes, at most they have cars to pursue you in. It isn't

that you know something bad could happen to you some-
day or if you go where you should not go, it's that you
see and know that the worst is happening to you right
now, the thing you most dread, and then the hunted man
doesn't drink or eat or stop either; or sometimes he does,
staying still more out of panic than from any certainty of
being safe and sheltered, more than a stillness, it's a paraly-
sis, like an insect that doesn't fly away or a soldier in his
trench. But even then he doesn't sleep except when exhaustion undermines what is happening right now and
deprives it of reality, when all the years of his former life re-
assert themselves — it takes so long for habits to fade, the
idea of an existence that isn't short-term — and he decides
for an instant that the present is the lie, the daydream or
nightmare, and rejects it for being so incongruent. Then
he sleeps and eats and drinks and has sex if he gets lucky or
pays, stops to chat for a bit, forgetting that the venomous
footsteps never stop and are always moving forward while
his own perpetually innocent feet are detained or don't
obey or might even be bare. And that's the worst thing, the
greatest danger; you must not forget that if you're fleeing
you can never take off your shoes or watch television, or
look into the eyes of someone who appears in front of you
and might hold your attention, my eyes only look back
while those of my pursuers look ahead, at my dark back,
and so they are bound to catch up with me always.

   It all happened because of Mr. Presley, and that is not
one of those idiotic lines referring to the record that was
playing the night we met, or to the time we were careless

and went too far, or to the idol of the person who caused the problem by forcing us to go to a concert to seduce her or just to make her happy. It all happened because of Elvis Presley in person, or Mr. Presley, as I used to call him until he told me it made him feel like his father. Everyone called him Elvis, just Elvis, with great familiarity, and that's what adoring fans and detractors alike still call him even after his death, people who never saw him in the flesh or exchanged a single word with him, or, back then, people who were meeting him for the first time, as if his fame had made him the involuntary friend or unwitting servant of one and all, and this may be normal and even justifiable, however much I disliked it, for the whole world already did know him even then, didn't they? And still does. Even so, I preferred to call him Mr. Presley and then Presley alone, by his surname, when he told me to drop the Mr. that made him feel so elderly, though I'm not sure he didn't later regret the request a little, I have a feeling he liked to hear himself called that at least once in his life, Mr. Presley or señor Presley, depending on the language, at the age of twenty-seven or twenty-eight. And that — the language or its decorative fringes, its most ornamental aspects — was what brought me to him, when I was hired to be part of his entourage of collaborators, assistants and advisers for what was supposed to be six weeks, that was how long it was supposed to take to shoot *Fun in Acapulco*, which I think came out in Spain under a different title, as usual, not *Diversión en Acapulco* or *Marcha en Acapulco* but *El ídolo en Acapulco*. I never saw it in Spain.

But here in Spain, not long ago, I did buy the record that went with it, the original soundtrack, which happened to catch my eye as I was looking for something by Previn. I got it because it made me laugh and brought back memories I'd once decided I would rather forget, just as everyone else in the crew had undoubtedly decided to forget them, and tried hard to forget them, and succeeded: the liner notes to the record once again trot out the old lie that has now been consecrated, the false history. The notes say that Presley never set foot in Acapulco during the making of the film, that all his scenes were shot at the Paramount Studios in Los Angeles to spare him the trouble and the trip, while a second unit crew went to Mexico to shoot landscape stills and footage of locals in the streets for use as backgrounds, Presley outlined against the sea and the beach, against the streets as he rides a bicycle with a boy perched on the handlebars, against the cliffs of La Perla, in front of the hotel where his character worked or wanted to work; he played a traumatized former trapeze artist named Mike Windgren, I always remember names, more than faces. The official version has prevailed, as happens with almost everything, but it is a highly doctored version, as official versions generally are, no matter who provides them, an individual or a government, the police or a movie studio. It's true that all the footage with Presley that actually appears in the film — as it was first shown and in the video version that exists today —

was shot in Hollywood, whenever Presley is on screen, and he's hardly ever offscreen in the whole film. They were very careful not to keep or use a single shot with him in it that hadn't been taken in the studios, not a single one that could have contradicted the official version given out by the producer and by señor Presley's entourage. But that doesn't mean there wasn't other footage which was cut, painstakingly and deliberately cut, in this case, and possibly fed to the flames or into the maw of a shredder, reduced to a celluloid pulp: not a trace must remain, not a millimeter, not a single frame, or that's what I imagine. Because the truth is that Presley did go to Mexico on location, not for three weeks but for ten days, at the end of which he not only abandoned the country without saying goodbye to anyone, but decided he had never been there, never set foot there, not for ten days or five or even one, Mr. Presley hadn't budged from California or Tennessee or Missouri or wherever it was, he hadn't set foot in Acapulco or in Mexico itself and the person who'd been interviewed and seen by tourists and Acapulqueños — or whatever they're called — during those days in February was simply one of his many doubles, who were as necessary or more necessary than ever for this production because Presley's character — in order to get over the nasty shock of having dropped his brother from a trapeze, with the consequent shattering of his morale and his flying brother's body (smashed to bits) — had to throw himself into the Pacific from the heights of the brutal cliffs of La Perla in the final or rather penultimate scene of *Fun in Acapulco,* a title on which no one had wasted any great mental energy. That was the official version of Presley's sojourn in Mexico, or rather his lack of a sojourn; it's still around, I see, which to some extent is understandable. Or perhaps it's simpler than that, perhaps it's just that there is never a way of erasing what's been said, true or false, once it's been said: accusations and inventions, slanders and stories and fabrications, disavowal is not enough, it doesn't erase but adds; once an event has been recounted there will be a thousand contradictory and impossible versions long, long before the event is annihilated: denials and discrepancies coexist with what they refute or deny, they accumulate, add up, they never cancel anything out but only end up sanctioning it for as long as people go on talking, the only way to erase is to say nothing, and go on saying nothing for a very long time.

Thirty-three years have gone by since it happened and eighteen since señor Presley died, and he is dead, though the whole world still knows and listens to and misses him. And it's the truth that I knew him in the flesh and we were in Acapulco, absolutely, he was there and I was there, and in Mexico City, where we flew more often than we should have in his private plane, trips that took hours, at ungodly hours of the night, he was there and I was there, though I was there longer, far too long, or so it seemed to me, a chase lasts like no other kind of time because every second counts, one, two and three and four, they haven't caught me yet, they haven't butchered me yet, here I am and I'm breathing, one, two and three and four.

Yes: we were there, we were all there, the film's entire crew and señor Presley's entire retinue, which was far more extensive, he traveled — well, "travel" may be an exaggeration: he moved — with a legion at his back, a battalion of more or less indispensable parasites, each with his own function or without any very precise function at all, lawyers, managers, make-up artists, musicians, hairstylists, vocal accompanists — the invariable Jordanaires — secretaries, trainers, sparring partners — his nostalgia for boxing — agents, image consultants, costume designers and a seamstress, sound technicians, drivers, electricians, pilots, financial expediters, publicists, promoters, press people, official and unofficial spokesmen, the president of his national fan club on an authorized inspection or delivering a report, and of course bodyguards, choreographers, a diction coach, mixing engineers, a teacher of facial and gestural expression (who wasn't able to do much), occasional doctors and nurses and an around-the-clock personal pharmacist with an implausible arsenal of remedies, I never saw such a medicine chest. Each, they claimed, was answerable to certain others in an organized hierarchy, but it was not at all easy to know who answered to whom nor how many divisions and subdivisions there were, how many departments and teams, you would have needed to draw up a family tree or that other thing, I mean a flow chart. There were individuals whom no

one was supervising at all closely — everyone thought
they were taking orders from someone else — people
who came and went and prowled and milled around
without anyone ever knowing exactly what their mission might be, though it was taken for granted that they
had a mission, back then no one was very suspicious,
Kennedy hadn't been assassinated yet. All of them had
the initials "EP" embroidered on their jackets, shirts, tee-
shirts, overalls or blouses, in blue, red, or white, depending on the color of the garment, and any overeager
bystander who asked his mother to do a little embroi-
dering for him could have passed himself off as a member of the crew without further difficulty. No one asked
questions back then, there were too many of us for
everyone to know everyone else, and I think the only
person who tried to keep an eye on things a little and su-
pervise the whole group was Colonel Tom Parker, Presley's discoverer, or tutor or godfather or something like
that, they told me (no one was particularly well-in-
formed about anything), and whose name appeared in
the credits of all Presley's films as "Technical Adviser," a
vague title if ever there was one. His appearance was
quite distinguished and severe and even somewhat mys-
terious in that motley setting; he was always well
dressed and wearing a tie, his jaw set tight as if he never
relaxed, his teeth clenched as if he ground them in his
sleep, and he spoke very softly but very sternly right in
the face of the person he was addressing, making sure
his listener was the only person who heard him even if

he were speaking in a room full of people, who were often whiling the time away in unbridled gossip. I'm not sure where the title of Colonel came from, whether he really had been in the army or if it was just a whim and he called himself Colonel in nominal fulfilment of some truncated aspiration. But if so, then what was to prevent him from calling himself General? His lean figure and carefully combed gray hair inspired respect and even apprehension in most people, so much so that when his presence made itself felt on the set or in an office or a room the place would begin to empty out, imperceptibly but rapidly, as if he were a man of ill omen, as if no one wanted to be exposed for long to his Nordic eye, a translucent eye, difficult to meet head-on. Though he wore civilian clothing and his demeanor was more senatorial than military, everyone, including Mr. Presley, always called him Colonel.

My own role was certainly not indispensable but resulted from one of Presley's caprices; I was hired just for that single occasion. And there we all were, the regulars of his formulaic movies, all copied from each other — *Fun* was the thirteenth — and the newcomers, all of us present for the indolent shooting of a ridiculous film, without rhyme or reason, at least in my opinion, I'm still amazed that the screenwriter was actually paid — a guy named Weiss who was clearly incapable of making the slightest effort, he hung around the set paying no attention to anything but the music, I mean the music Presley sang at the drop of a hat, with his inseparable Jordanaires or another group of vocal accompanists who went by the offensive name of The Four Amigos. I don't really know what the plot of the film was supposed to be, and not because it was too complicated; on the contrary, it's hard to follow a plot when there is no story line and no style to substitute for one or distract you; even later, after seeing the film — before the premiere there was a private screening — I can't tell you what its excuse for a plot was. All I know is that Elvis Presley, the tortured former trapeze artist, as I said — but he's only tortured sometimes, he also spends a lot of time going swimming, perfectly at ease, and uninhibitedly romancing women — wanders around Acapulco, I don't remember why, let's say he's trying to shake off his dark past or he's on the run from the FBI, perhaps some thought the fratricide was deliberate (I'm not at all clear on that and I could be mixing up my movies, thirty-three years have gone by). As is logical and necessary, Elvis sings and dances in various places: a cantina, a hotel, a terrace facing the daunting cliff. From time to time he stares, with envy and some kind of complex, at the swimmers — or rather, divers — who plunge into the pool with tremendous smugness from a diving board of only average height. There's a lady bullfighter, a local, who has a thing for Elvis, and another woman, the hotel's publicist or something like that, who competes with the matadora for him, Mr. Presley was always very successful with the women, in fiction as in life. There's also a Mexican rival named Moreno who jumps off the diving board far too often, frenetically, pausing only to taunt Windgren and call him a coward. Presley competes with him for the publicist, who is none other than the Swiss actress Ursula Andress, in a bikini or with her shirt capriciously knotted across her midriff and ribbons winding through her wet hair, she had just made herself universally desirable and famous — particularly among teenage boys — by appearing in a white bikini in the first James Bond adventure, *Agente 007 contra el doctor No,* or whatever it was called in Spain; her Acapulcan bikinis weren't cut very high and didn't live up to expectations, they were far more chaste than the one she wore in Jamaica, Colonel Tom Parker may have insisted, he seemed to be a gentleman of some decorum or maybe he was unwilling to tolerate any unfair competition with his protégé. Running around somewhere in all that was also a pseudo-Mexican boy, greatly overendowed with the gift of gab, whom Windgren befriended — the two amigos — without knowing why or for what purpose: that boy was an epidemic of talk and was absolutely to be avoided and ignored even in the elevators, which in fact was what we all did every time he came chattering towards us imagining that the fiction carried over into life, since in the movie he was a boon companion to the former trapeze artist embittered by the fraternal fatality and by Moreno the mean diving champ. That was the whole story, if you can call that a story.

And somewhere in there, very depressed, were also two veterans of the cinema whose attitude, between skeptical and humiliated, contrasted with the festive atmosphere of that thirteenth production. (We should have thought more about that number.) One was the director Richard Thorpe; the other, the actor Paul Lukas, a native of Hungary whose real name was Lukács. Thorpe was about seventy years old and Lukas around eighty, and both found themselves at the end of their careers playing the fool in Acapulco. Thorpe was a goodhearted and patient man, or, rather, a heartsick and defeated man, and he directed with little enthusiasm, as if only a pistol shoved into the back of his neck by Parker could convince him to shout "Action" before each shot. "Cut," though, he would say more energetically, and with relief. He had made terrific, very worthwhile adventure movies like *Ivanhoe, Knights of the Round Table, All the Brothers Were Valiant,* and *The House of the Seven Hawks* and *Quentin Durward,* and had even worked with Presley on his third film, back in less formulaic days, directing *Jailhouse Rock, El rock de la cárcel,* "that was something else altogether, in black and white," he rationalized to Lukas during a break in the shooting; but discreetly, he wasn't a man to offend anyone, not even the provincial magnate McGraw or the producer Hal Wallis, who was also well along in years. As for Lukas or Lukács himself, he had almost always played supporting roles, but he had an Oscar under his belt and had taken orders from Cukor and Hitchcock, Minelli and Huston, Tourneur and Walsh, Whale and Mamoulian and Wyler, and those names were permanently on his lips as if he wanted their noble memory to conjure away the ignominy of what he was afraid would be his final role: in *Fun in Acapulco* he played Ursula Andress's vaguely European father, a diplomat or government minister or perhaps an aristocrat come down so far in the world that he now worked as a chef at the hotel. During the entire shoot he never had a single chance to take off the lofty white hat — far too tall, it had to be starched stiff to stay up — that is the cliché of that profession, at least while he was on the set, I mean, mouthing trite phrases that embarrassed him, but as soon as Thorpe mumbled "Cut" with a yawn, and even if another take was being shot immediately, Paul Lukas would tear off the loathsome headgear in a rage, looking at it with a disdain that may have been uniquely Hungarian — in any case, an emotion never seen in America — and muttering audibly, "Not a single shot, dear God, at my age, not one shot of my glistening pate." I was glad to learn two years later that this was only his penultimate film; he was able to bid his profession adieu with a great role and an excellent performance, that of the good Mr. Stein in *Lord Jim*, along with true peers such as Eli Wallach and James Mason. He was always polite to me and it would have pained him to say his farewell to the cinema at Mr. Presley's side.

It must not be inferred from this that I've ever looked down or now look down on Mr. Presley. On the contrary. There can't be many people who have admired him and still admire him more than I do (though without fanaticism), and I know I have enormous competition in that. There's never been another voice like his, another singer with so much talent and such a range, and also he was a pleasant, good-natured man, far less conceited than he had every right to be. But movies... no. He started out taking them seriously, and his earliest films weren't bad, *King Creole* for example (he admired James Dean so much that he knew all his parts by heart). But Mr. Presley's problem, which is the problem of many people who are uncommonly successful, was the boundless extravagance it forced him to: the more success someone has and the more money he makes, the more work and the less freedom he has. Maybe it's because of all the other people who are also making money from him and therefore exploit him, force him to produce, compose, write, paint or sing, squeeze him and emotionally blackmail him with their friendship, their influence, their pleas, since threats aren't very effective against someone who's at the top. Then again, there can always be threats; that's a given. So Elvis Presley had made twelve films in six years, in addition to multiplying himself in a thousand other varied activities; at the end of the day, the movies were only a secondary industry in his conglomerate. Behind this kind of person there are always businessmen and promoters who have trouble accepting that from time to time the manufacturer of what they sell stops making it. The fact is, I've never seen anyone who was as exploited as Mr. Presley, anyone who put out so much, and if he wanted to avoid it he wasn't helped by his nature, which wasn't

Javier Marías

bad or surly or even arrogant—a little belligerent at times, yes—but obliging; it was hard for him to say no or put up much opposition. So his films got worse and worse, and Presley had to make himself more and more laughable in them, which was not very gratifying for someone who admired him as much as I did to see.

He wasn't aware of it, or so it seemed; if he was, he accepted the ridiculousness without making any faces about it and even with a touch of pride, it was all part of the job. And since he was a hard and serious and even enthusiastic worker, he couldn't see how his roles looked from the outside or make fun of them. I imagine it was in the same disciplined and pliant frame of mind that he allowed himself to grow drooping sideburns in the seventies and agreed to appear on stage tricked out like a circus side show, wearing suits bedecked with copious sequins and fringes, bell bottoms slit up the side, belts as wide as a novice whore's, high-heeled goblin boots, and a short cape—a cape—that made him look more like Super Rat than whatever he was probably trying for, Superman, I would imagine. Fortunately I didn't have any dealings with him during that period, not even for ten days, and in the sixties when I knew him he didn't have to stoop so low, but neither was he free of all the extravagant notions that happened to occur to other people, and I'm afraid it was in *Fun in Acapulco* that he got stuck with the worst of those bright ideas.

Every time I watched them shooting a scene I thought, "Oh no, my God, not that, señor Presley," and the amazing thing was that none of it seemed to bother Mr. Presley, he even, with his undoubted capacity for kidding around, enjoyed the horror. I don't think he was pleased or proud; it was just that he didn't have the heart to raise objections or make negative comments that would disappoint whoever it was who had come up with today's delirious concept, whether it was Colonel Tom Parker or the choreographer, O'Curran, or the producer Hal Wallis himself, or even that quartet with the objectionable name, The Four Amigos, whose flashes of inspiration came in pairs. Or maybe he had so much confidence in his own talent that he thought he could emerge unscathed from any fiasco; certainly in the course of his career he sang about everything and in all languages — for which he had no gift whatsoever — without any resultant collapse of his reputation. But we didn't know that yet. "Oh no, dear God, spare him that," I thought when I found out that Presley was going to play the tambourine and do a Mexican sombrero dance in a cantina surrounded by folkloric mariachis — one group was the Mariachi Aguila, the other the Mariachi Los Vaqueros, I couldn't tell them apart — while he sang *"Vino, dinero y amor,"* everyone joining in on the chorus. "Oh Lord, don't let it happen," I thought when they announced that Mr. Presley would have to wear a short, tight jacket with a frilled shirt and scarlet cummerbund to sing the solemn *"El Toro"* while stamping like a flamenco dancer. "Oh no, please, what will his father think," I thought as he perpetrated "And the Bullfighter Was a Lady" wearing some approximation of a Mexican rancher's garb and swirling a bullfighter's cape over his carefully coiffed head or throwing it around his shoulders with the yellow side up as if it were a cloak. "Oh no, that's going too far, that's regicide," I thought when I read in the screenplay that in the final scene Presley was to sing "Guadalajara," in Spanish, at the edge of the cliff, cheered on insincerely by all the mariachis together. But that's another story, and the linguistic disaster was no fault of mine.

That was what they hired me for. Not just to avoid linguistic disaster, much more than that: everything was to be pedantically perfect. I'd been in Hollywood a couple of months, doing whatever came my way, I'd arrived with some letters of recommendation from Edgar Neville, whom I knew a little bit in Madrid. The letters weren't very useful—almost all his friends were dead or retired—but at least they allowed me to make a few contacts and stave off starvation for the time being. I was offered little jobs lasting a week or two, on location or at a studio, as an extra or an errand boy, whatever came up, I was twenty-two years old. So I couldn't believe it when Hal Pereira called me to his office and said, "Hey, Roy, you're Spanish, from Spain, right?"

My last name, Ruibérriz, isn't easy for English speakers, so I quickly became Roy Berry, and people called me Roy, that was my Christian name over there, or first name, as they say, and I appear as Roy Berry, in tiny letters, in the credits of certain films made in '62 and '63, I'd prefer not to say which ones.

"Yes sir, Mr. Pereira, I'm from Madrid, Spain," I answered.

"Terrific. Listen. I've got something fantastic for you and you'll be getting us out of a last-minute jam. Six weeks in Acapulco; well, three there and three here. Movie with Elvis Presley. *Holiday in Acapulco*" — that was the initial title, no one was ever prepared to tax their brain in any way over that film — "He's a lifeguard, trapeze artist, I'm not sure, I'm joining up tomorrow. Elvis has to talk and sing a little in Spanish, right? Then suddenly he drops this bomb on us, claiming he doesn't want to have a Mexican accent; he wants it to be pure Spanish as if he learned it in Seville, says he found out they pronounce the letter *c* differently in Spain and that's how he wants to pronounce it, O.K., you're the one who knows about that. So the ten million Mexicans we've got swarming around here are no use at all, he wants a Spaniard from Spain to stay with him through the entire shoot and take charge of his classy accent. We don't have many of those around here, Spaniards from Spain; what do we need them for? It's ridiculous. But Elvis is Elvis. We won't take no for an answer. You'll be hired by his team, and you'll take your orders from him, not us. But Paramount will pay you; Elvis is Elvis. So don't expect to make any more than what you're making this week. What do you say. We're leaving tomorrow."

There was nothing to say, or rather, I was speechless. Six weeks of easy, safe work, at the side of an idol, and in Acapulco to top it all off. I think that for the first and last time I blessed the place of my birth, which doesn't usually bring me any advantages, and there I went, off to Mexico, to do hardly anything, since Mr. Presley had to pronounce very few Spanish phrases in the course of the film, things like "muchas muchachas bonitas," "amigo," and "gracias." The hardest part was "Guadalajara," he had to sing the whole song with the original lyrics, but that was scheduled for the third week of the shoot and there would be plenty of time to practice.

Mr. Presley won me over right away, he was a funny, friendly man and after all he was only five or six years older than me though at that age even five or six years is enough for the younger one to be in awe of the more experienced, and even more so if the older one is already legendary. The concern with his accent was no more than a passing whim, and as it turned out he was completely incapable of pronouncing the Madrid *c*, so we settled for the Seville *c*; I promised him that this was indeed the famous Spanish *c*, though he found it suspiciously similar to the Mexican *c*, which, as a matter of principle, he wanted to avoid. I ended up being employed more as an interpreter than as a professor of Spanish diction.

He was restless and needed to be doing something all the time, he had to get out of Acapulco as soon as the day's filming was over, so we would take his plane and a few of us would go to Mexico City — five of us could fit, including the pilot, it was a small plane, the five amigos — or we would all go in several cars to Petatlán or Copala, Presley couldn't stand to spend the day and the night in the same place, though he also got tired of the new place right away and we always went back a few hours later, and sometimes a few minutes later if he didn't like what he saw, maybe it was only the trip that appealed to him. But he also had to work the next morning, and what with all the to and fro we would sleep from two or three a.m. to seven; after three or four days of that the rest of the excursionists were worn out, but not Presley, his endurance was incomparable, a man in a perpetual state of explosion, used to giving concerts. He spent the whole day singing or crooning, even when he was under no professional obligation to do so, you could see he had a passion for it, he was a singing machine, endlessly rehearsing with The Jordanaires or the mariachis or even The Four Amigos, and in the plane or the car, if conversation hadn't set in, it wouldn't be long before he started humming and the rest of us would join him, it was an honor to sing with Presley, though I hit a lot of false notes and he would laugh and gleefully encourage me, "Go on, Roy, go on, just you by yourself, you've got a great career ahead of you." (We switched back and forth between slow and fast numbers, and I've sung along with him above the clouds of Mexico on one of my favorites, "Don't," and on "Teddy Bear" — *PA-palala, PA-palala* —. You don't forget a thing like that.) His mania for singing made everyone involved in the shoot a little frenetic, or at least excited, Wallis's people and Presley's people, no one can take a life of non-stop music in stride, I mean without being a musician. Even the good Paul Lukas, at his advanced age and with his great burden of annoyance, hummed at times without realizing it, I once heard him humming "Bossa Nova Baby" between his teeth, though in his defense that song really sticks in your mind, I'm sure he didn't realize what he was doing. Presley sang it with a bunch of guys in glittering green jackets shaking tambourines.

But most unbearable of all were the kind of people who not only let themselves be carried along on the tide of song and incessant humming, but who went looking for it and egged Mr. Presley on in order to feel they were on his level or to ingratiate themselves, trying to out-Elvis Elvis. There were a number of them among that vast company, but the most grotesque of all was McGraw, the small-town magnate, a man of about fifty-five — my age now, awful thought — who, during the days he spent on location with us, behaved not like a young man of twenty-seven (Presley's age) or twenty-two (mine) but like a fourteen-year-old in the full frenzy of burgeoning pubescence. George McGraw was one of the many inappropriate individuals who swam along in Presley's wake for reasons that were not at all clear, maybe they were big investors in his conglomerate, or people from his home town whom he tolerated for that reason or owed old favors to, like Colonel Tom Parker, possibly. I found out that George McGraw had several businesses in Mississippi and maybe in Alabama and Tennessee, but in any case in Tupelo, where Presley was born. He was one of those overbearing types who are incapable of rectifying their despotic manners even if they're very far from the five-hundred-square-mile area where their remote and doubtless crooked business dealings matter. He was the owner of a newspaper in Tuscaloosa or Chattanooga or even in Tupelo itself, I don't remember, all of those places were often on his lips. It seemed he had tried to make the city in question change its name to Georgeville, and, having failed in that ambition, he refused to give his newspaper the town's name and christened it instead with his own first name: *The George Herald* no less, in daily typographic retaliation. That was what some people called him in derision, George Herald, reducing him to a messenger (I've known other men like him since: editors, producers, cultural businessmen who quickly lose the adjective and are left with the noun). I remember joking with Mr. Presley about those towns in his native region, he thought it was hilarious when I told him what Tupelo means in Spanish if you divide the first two syllables ("your hair," he repeated, laughing uproariously), especially since it sounds so much like toupee. "They seem completely made up, those names," I told him, "Tuscaloosa sounds like a kind of liquor and Chattanooga like a dance, let's go have a couple of tuscaloosas and dance the chattanooga," with Mr. Presley everything went fine if you joked around a lot, he was a cheerful man with a quick, easy laugh, maybe too quick and too easy, one of those people who are so undemanding that they take to everyone, even airheads and imbeciles. This can be a little irritating, but you can't really get angry with that kind of simple soul. And anyway, I was on the payroll.

George Herald, I mean McGraw, was no doubt very boastful of his friendship with Presley and would imitate him in the most pathetic way: he wore a sorry excuse for a toupee, an overly compact mass that looked like Davy Crockett's coonskin cap from the front, and from the side, since there was no tail, like a bellboy's hat, though without the chin strap. He admired or envied Presley so much that he wanted to be more than Presley, he didn't want to lag behind in any respect, but to be a kind of paternalistic partner, as if the two of them were singers at the same level of success and he were the more experienced and dominant. Except that McGraw couldn't sing at all (even in the airborne choruses of that ill-fated journey which for me was the last), and his ability to rival Elvis was no less delusional. He would shamelessly appropriate Elvis's phrases, so that if Elvis said to the pilot and me one afternoon, "Come on, Roy, Hank, let's go to FD," referring to Mexico City, Federal District in his language, and then added: "FD sounds like a tribute to Fats Domino, let's go to Fats Domino" (whom he admired tremendously), McGraw would repeat the quip a hundred times until he had entirely stripped it of any conceivable charm: "We're off to see Fats Domino, to Fats Domino we go." You start to hate the joke. In the throes of this half-adulatory, half-competitive zeal, he spent the two days of his visit exaggeratedly tripping the light fantastic wherever he happened to be (on the beach, in the hotel, in a restaurant, in an elevator, in what was supposed to be a business meeting) as soon as he heard a few notes nearby or even in the distance, and there was always music playing somewhere. He danced in the most unseemly fashion, doing a big loco act, aided and abetted by a towel which he rubbed at top speed against his shoulders or along the backs of his thighs as if he were a stripper, it was truly a vile spectacle since he was husky verging on fat but moved like a hysterical teenager, shaking that broad head from which not one of his Davy Crockett hairs ever came unglued, and spinning his tiny feet like tornadoes. And he did not stop. In the plane, on the way out (for me there was no return trip), we had to ask Presley not to sing anything that was too fast, because the owner of the *George Herald* would immediately go into his dance fever — those wee vicious eyes of his — and endanger our airborne equilibrium. McGraw didn't like slow tunes, only "Hound Dog," "All Shook Up," "Blue Suede Shoes" and so on, songs that let him go nuts and do his number with the towel or whatever scarf or handkerchief happened to be at hand, his indecent bump and grind. It may be that he was what we would call in Spanish today *un criptogay*, a homosexual who hides it even from himself, but he boasted of never letting a tasty chick — his expression — get away from him without putting his hands on her or making some lewd remark.

That night, in addition to Presley, on whom he was always pathologically fixated, he had his eye on an actress, very young, very blonde, who played a bit part in the film and who happened to come along on this particular expedition to the DF; I always went along to act as interpreter, Hank could get out of it when we went by car.

But that night we were flying. The girl was named Terry, or Sherry, the name has gotten away from me, it's strange, or not so strange, and McGraw had the gall to compete in that arena, too, with Presley, I mean he was putting the moves on her without waiting to see if the King had any plans in that respect, which was a serious lapse in manners in addition to being idiotically oblivious, since it was clear to one and all that the young lady had ideas of her own which in no way included the moronic magnate.

It wasn't Presley's fault, or mine, except secondarily, it was primarily McGraw's fault, and for that reason alone have I spoken, very much against my will, of that fake frontiersman. When the five of us walked into a dance hall or disco or cantina — five if we had flown to Mexico City; ten or fifteen if we were in Acapulco, Petatlán, or Copala — a riot would usually break out the moment those present realized that Presley was there, and women would be fainting all over the place. As soon as the owners or managers realized he was there they would put an end to the commotion the more bold-hearted girls were making and throw out the swooners so Elvis wouldn't get annoyed and leave right away — I've seen night club bouncers scaring off harmless teenage girls with their fists, we didn't like it but there was nothing else to do if we wanted to have a quiet tuscaloosa or watch a chattanooga — and once order had been reestablished, what generally happened was that all eyes without exception were on us, to the great detriment of whatever show was being performed on stage, and nothing ever went any further than that and a few furtive autographs. Once we had a kind of fore-warning of what would happen that night, a few young fellows got jealous; they started trying to provoke us and made some seriously inappropriate remarks. I de-cided it was best not to translate any of it for Mr. Presley and convinced him to get out of there, and nothing hap-pened. Those guys had knives, and sometimes you see the capataz embodied in anyone with a bulging wallet.

We happened to wander into an inhospitable and not very well-policed joint, or else the thugs inside were there to protect the owners rather than any patron, even if he happened to be a famous gringo. We would gener-ally stop in wherever we felt like it, going on how the dive looked from the outside and what its posters prom-ised, pictures of singers or dancers, almost always Mex-ican, a few unconvincingly Brazilian women. There were quite a lot of people inside, in an atmosphere that had a listless, thuggish savor to it, but it was the third stop of the evening and we hadn't been stinting on tequila, so we went over to the bar and stood there all in a row, making room for ourselves in a way that wasn't exactly the height of good manners, but anything else would have been out of place.

Across the dance floor was an eye-catching table of seven or eight people, who looked as if they had a lot of money if not a lot of class, five men with three women who may have been rented for the night or hired on a

daily basis, and both the men and the women were star-
ing at us fixedly despite the fact that we had our backs to
the dance floor and to their table. Maybe they were just
guys who liked to watch other people dancing from up
close; the women danced, but among the men only one
did, the youngest, a limber individual with high cheekbones and the look of a bodyguard, a look he shared
with two others who stood by and never left their
bosses alone for a second. They didn't appear to have
any connection to the place, but it turned out they did,
and so did one of their bosses; he was a common
enough type in Mexico, around thirty-five with a moustache and curly hair, but in Hollywood they would immediately have put him under contract as a new
Ricardo Montalbán or Gilbert Roland or César Romero,
he was tall and handsome and had neatly rolled up his
shirtsleeves very high, displaying his biceps which he
constantly flexed. His partner, or whatever he was, was
fat with a very fair complexion, more European blood
there, his hair combed straight back in a dandified way
and too long at the nape of the neck, but he didn't dye it
to take out the gray. Nowadays we'd call them mafiosos
lavados, "whitewashed gangsters," but that expression
wasn't in use then: they were intimidating but for the
time being irreproachable, owners of restaurants or
stores or bars or even ranches, businessmen with employees who accompanied them wherever they went
and protected them when necessary from their peons
or even from some angered capataz. In his hand the fat

man had a vast green handkerchief that he used, by turns, to mop his brow or to fan the atmosphere as if he were shooing flies away or performing magic tricks, sending it floating out over the dance floor for a second.

Our arrival hadn't created much of a stir because we had our backs to the room and because Hank, who was enormous, stood, looking very dissuasive, between Mr. Presley and the three or four women who first came up to us. After a few minutes, Presley spun around on his bar stool and looked out at the dance floor; there was a murmur, he drank as if nothing were going on, and the buzz diminished. He had a certain glassy look that could sometimes appease a crowd, it was as if he didn't see them and canceled them out, or he would shift his expression slightly in a way that seemed to promise something good for later on. He himself was calm just then, drinking from his glass and, watching the hermanos Mexicanos dancing, sometimes a kind of a melancholy came over him. It didn't last.

But there was no stopping the exasperating George McGraw, who of course was relentless when it came to making demonstrations of his own prowess; if he saw Presley in a moment of calm, far from adapting to the mood or following his lead, he would seize on it to try to outshine and eclipse him — fat chance. He wanted Sherry to dance, practically threatened her, but she didn't go with him to the dance floor and made a crude gesture, plugging her nose as if to say that something stank, and I saw that this did not pass unnoticed by the fat guy with the oiled-back locks, who wrinkled his brow, or by the new César Montalbán or Ricardo Roland, who flexed his right bicep even higher than usual.

So McGraw got out on the floor, swaying his hips and taking very short little steps all by himself, his button eyes ablaze with the trumpeting rumba that was playing, and he couldn't keep from displaying his repertory of dreadful movements or from emitting sharp, ill-timed cries that were a mockery of the way Mexicans shout to urge someone on. Hank and Presley were watching him in amusement; they burst out laughing and young Sherry started laughing too, out of contagion and flirtation. The owner of the *George Herald* was dancing so obscenely that his crazed thrusts of the hip were getting in the way of some of the women on the dance floor; the bodyguard with high cheekbones who moved as if he were made of rubber shot him dead with a glance from his Indian eyes, but nothing stopped him. The other dancers did stop and stood aside, whether out of disgust or in order to get a better view of McGraw I don't know: he was giving his trapper's or bellhop's cap such a vigorous shaking that I was afraid it would go sailing off and come to a bad end, forgetting that he wore it securely glued to his scalp. The problem was that he didn't travel with his towel, and he must have considered it an indispensable element in his dance routine; consequently, as the pale-skinned fat man, in a moment of carelessness, flung his handkerchief up to aerate the atmosphere, McGraw filched it from him without so much as a glance and immediately flung it over his shoulders, holding it by the two ends, and rubbing it against himself, up and down, with the customary celerity that by then we had seen all too often. The fat man kept his limp hand extended during the moment following the loss, he didn't pull it back right away as if he hadn't given up on recovering his beloved green handkerchief — some kind of a fetish maybe. In fact, he tried to reach it from his seat when McGraw came his way in his increasingly indecorous dance. What finally made the fat man lose patience was a moment in McGraw's sashayings when he both withheld the handkerchief and started voluptuously toweling it across his buttocks. The fat man stood up for a second — he was a very tall fat man, I saw — and angrily grabbed the handkerchief away from the dancing fool. But the dancer gave an agile spin and, before the fat man had resumed his seat, snatched the handkerchief back again with an imperious gesture, he was used to having his way and having his orders followed back in Tupelo or Tuscaloosa. It was a comical moment, but I wasn't happy to see that Gilbert Romero and his crowd were not at all amused, because it really was funny, the fat man and the semi-fat man quarreling over the green silk at the edge of the dance floor. I was even less happy to see what happened next: the impatient expression on the stiff-haired fat man's face changed to brutal cold rage, and he seized the handkerchief back from McGraw with a swipe of his big hand just at the moment the elastic bodyguard delivered a blow to the magnate's kidneys which made him fall to his knees, his dance stopped dead. As if he were well-rehearsed at this sort of gesture—but how could he be?—the fat man's next swift move was to twist the handkerchief around the kneeling McGraw's neck and start pulling on the ends to strangle him right then and there. In a second the cloth lost all its glide and stretched thin and unbelievably taut, like a slender cord, and its green color disappeared, a cord that was tightening. The fat man pulled hard on the two ends, his complexion red as a steak and his expression heartless, like a man tying up a clumsy package hurriedly and mechanically. I thought he was killing McGraw on the spot, like a flash of lightning and without saying a word, in front of a hundred witnesses on the dance floor, which in an instant emptied out completely. I admit I didn't know how to react, or maybe I felt fleetingly that at last we would be free of the small-town tycoon, and I did no more than think (or else the thought came later, but I attribute it to that moment): "He's killing him, killing him, he is killing him, no one could have seen it coming, death can be as stupid and unexpected as they say, you walk into some dive without ever imagining that everything can end there in the most ridiculous way and in a second, one, two and three and four, and every second that passes without anyone intervening makes this irreversible death more certain, the death that is happening as we watch, a rich man from Chattanooga being killed by a fat man with a bad nature in Mexico City right before our eyes."

Then I saw myself shouting something in Spanish out on the dance floor, all of us were there, Presley grabbing the lapels of the rubber man who twisted out of reach with a hard slap, Hank with the handkerchief in his hand, he had given the fat man a shove that sent him flying back to his seat and sent all the glasses on Roland's table crashing. This crew wasn't carrying knives, or not just knives, they were full-grown men, not peons but capatazes and landowners, and they carried pistols, I could see it in the way the other two thugs moved, one at the chest and the other on the hip, though Montalbán restrained them, opening out a horizontal hand as if to say, "Five." Hank was the most excited, he always carried a pistol, too, though fortunately he hadn't put his hand on it, a man with a gun gets more excited when he sees he may be using it. He wadded the handkerchief into a ball and threw it at the hotheaded fat man, saying in English, "Are you crazy or what? You could have killed him." The silk floated in its journey.

"¿Qué ha dicho ese?" Romero asked me immediately, he had already realized I was the only member of the group who spoke the language.

"Que si está loco, ha podido matarlo," I answered automatically. "No es para tanto," I added on my own account. What *was* the big deal?

It was all coming to nothing, every second that went by now, every panting breath we all drew made the tension diminish, an altercation of no importance whatsoever, the music, the heat, the tequila, a foreigner who behaved like a spoiled brat, he was standing up now with

35

Sherry's help, coughing violently, he looked scared, unable to comprehend that anyone could possibly have harmed him. He was all right, either there hadn't been time for much harm to be done or the fat man wasn't as strong as he looked.

"La nena vieja se puso pesada con el amigo Julio y Julio se cansa pronto," said Romero Ricardo. "Será mejor que se la lleven rápido. Váyanse todos, las copas están pagadas."

"What did he say?" Presley asked me immediately. He had his own urgent need to understand, to know what was happening and what was being said, I saw him slipping into belligerence, the ghost of James Dean descended upon him and sent a shiver down my spine. His own movies were too bland to satisfy that ghost. Hank jerked his head toward the door.

"That we should get out of here fast. The drinks are on them."

"And what else? He said something else."

"He insulted Mr. McGraw, that's all."

Elvis Presley was a good friend to his friends, at least to his old friends, he had a sense of loyalty and a lot of pride and it had been many years since he had taken orders from anyone. It's only a short step from melancholy to brawling. And there was his nostalgia for boxing.

"Insulted him. That guy insulted him. First they try to kill him, then they insult him. What did he say? Come on, what did he say? And who is he to tell us to get out of here anyway?"

"¿Qué ha dicho?" now it was Roland César's turn to ask me. Their inability to understand each other was enraging them, a thing like that can really grate on your nerves in an argument.

"Que quién es usted para decir que nos vayamos."

"Han oido, Julio, muchachos, me pregunta el gachupín que quién soy yo para ponerlos en la calle," Montalbán answered without looking at me. I thought (if there was time for such a thought) that it was odd that he said I was the one asking who he was: it was Presley who was asking and I was only translating, it was a warning I didn't pay attention to, or that I picked up on too late, when you relive what happened, or reconstruct it. "Soy aquí el propietario. Aquí soy el dueño, por muy famoso que sea su patron," he repeated with a slight tremor of one of his mobile biceps. If he was the owner, as he claimed, he was very unfriendly, my boss didn't impress him, they hadn't come over to say hello when we came in and now they were throwing us out. "Y les digo que se larguen y se lleven a la bailona. La quiero ya fuera de mi vista, no espero."

"What did he say?" It was Presley's turn.

I was getting tired of the double onslaught of this crossfire. I looked at McGraw, la bailona, as Romero had called him, he was breathing more easily now but was still terrified — the tiny psychotic eyes were glazed — he was pulling at Hank's jacket to get us to leave, Hank was still making gestures with his head tilted towards Presley, Sherry was already heading for the door, McGraw leaning on her, maybe taking advantage, he was one of those guys who never learns. Fat Julio was in his seat, he had recovered his composure after his exertions, his whiteness had returned like a mask, he was following the conversational match with his hands crossed (rings glinting), like one who has not abandoned the idea of re-entering the fray.

Before answering Presley I thought it was a good idea for me to say something to Ricardo: "El no es quien usted cree. Es su doble, sabe, su sosias, para hacer las escenas de peligro en el cine, estamos rodando una película allí en Acapulco. Se llama Mike."

"El parecido es tan logrado," Julio interrupted sarcastically, "que le habrán hecho la cirugía estética a Mike, como a las presumidas." He wiped the by now utterly revolting handkerchief across his forehead.

"What did they say?" Presley insisted. "What did they say?"

I turned toward him.

"They're the owners. We'd better go."

"And what else? What were you saying about Mike? Who's Mike?"

"Mike is you, I told them that was your name, that you're your double, not yourself, but I don't think they believe me."

"And what did they say about George? You said they insulted him. Tell me what those guys said about George, they can't get away with just saying whatever they want."

This last comment was a genuine piece of North American naiveté. And that was where my share of the blame came in, though Presley and I were to blame only in the second place; the guilty party was primarily Mc-Graw, and maybe I was only to blame in the third place. How could I explain to Mr. Presley, at that moment, that the tough guys were using nouns in the feminine gender to refer to McGraw, la nena vieja, pesada, bailona, English nouns have no gender and I wasn't about to give him a Spanish lesson right there on that dance floor. I glanced over at la nena vieja, la bailona — I'm the same age now that he was then — he was smiling weakly, walking away, the coward, he was starting to feel as if he were out of danger, he was tugging at Hank, Hank was tugging a little at Presley ("Let's go, Elvis, it doesn't matter"), no one was tugging at me. I gestured my head towards César Gilbert.

"O.K. He called Mr. McGraw a fat faggot," I said. I couldn't avoid putting it like that, and I couldn't help saying it, I wanted the owner of the *Herald* to hear it and not be able to make any display of despotism or punish anyone or do anything except swallow the insult. And I wanted the others to hear it, pure childishness.

But I hadn't been thinking about what a stickler Presley was and for an instant I'd forgotten the ghost. We'd all been drinking tequila. Mr. Presley raised one finger, pointed it at me dramatically and said, "You're going to repeat this word for word, Roy, to the guy with the moustache, don't you leave out one syllable. Tell him this: you are a goon and a pig, and the only fat faggot here is your little girlfriend there with the handkerchief." That was what he said, with that way of twisting his mouth he sometimes had that inspired distrust in the mothers of his youngest fans. His insults were a little on the schoolboy side, nothing about sons of bitches or motherfuckers, words that had more weight in the sixties. He paused for a second, and then, with his finger still pointing, added, "Say that to him."

And I did say that to Ricardo César, I said it in Spanish (stammering a little): "Usted es un matón y un cerdo, y la única maricona gorda es su amiguita del pañuelo." As soon as I said "maricona gorda," translating my own words, "fat faggot," into Spanish, I realized it was the first time those exact words had been spoken there, really, though they weren't much more offensive than "bailona" or "nena vieja."

Presley went on: "Tell him this, too: We're leaving now because we want to and because this place stinks, and I hope someone sets fire to it soon, with all of you inside. Say that, Roy."

And I repeated in Spanish (but in a less wounding tone and a softer voice): "Ahora nos vamos porque queremos y porque este lugar apesta, y espero que se lo quemen pronto con todos ustedes dentro."

I saw how Gilbert Ricardo's biceps were quivering like jelly and a corner of his moustache twitched, I saw fat Julio open his mouth like a fish in feigned horror and run his fingers across his rings as if they were weapons,

I saw that one of the two thugs at the table openly pulled back the front of his jacket to exhibit the butt of a pistol in its holster, like an old print of one of Pancho Villa's men. But Ricardo Romero stretched out his hand to the horizon again, as if he were indicating "five," which was not at all comforting because there were five of us. Then, with the same hand, he briefly signaled to me with the index finger pointing upward, as if he were holding a pistol and his thumb were the raised safety. Sherry was at the door by then, along with McGraw whose hand was clutching his damaged loin, Hank was pulling at Presley with one hand and kept the other in his pocket, as if he were gripping something. I already said that no one was pulling at me.

Presley turned around when he saw I had translated everything, and in two shakes he was there with the others at the door, and the meaning of the way Hank had his hand in his jacket was unmistakable, to the Mexicans, too. I followed them, the door was already open — I was the straggler, all of them were walking outside, quickening their step, they were already out — I was about to go after them, but the rubber man shoved in between Presley and me, his back in front of my face, he was taller and blocked the others from sight for a second, then the rubber man went out with them, and the bouncer who'd been standing at the door keeping an eye on the street came in and closed it before I could get through. He stood in my way and kept me from passing.

"Tú, gachupín, te quedas."

41

I had never believed it was really true that we Spaniards are known as gachupines in Mexico, just as I never believed the other thing they told us when we were kids, that if you were ever in Mexico and ordered "una copita de ojén" — an anisette — to the rhythm of seven thumps on the bar of a cantina — or even if you thumped rhythmically seven times and didn't say a thing — they'd open fire on you without further ado because it was an insult. It didn't occur to me to try and verify this just then, I didn't much feel like having an anisette, or anything else.

This time it wasn't Gilbert Montalbán who called me gachupín but Julio, and he was looking more irate and uncontrolled to me, I'd watched him knotting up.

"Pero mis amigos ya se marchan," I said, turning around, "I have to go with them. No hablan español, you saw."

"Don't worry about that. Pacheco will go with them back to the hotel, they'll arrive safe and sound. But they'll never come back here, eso es seguro."

"They'll come back for me if you don't let me leave," I answered, trying to glance furtively back at the door, which did not open.

"No, they won't be back, they won't know the way," it was César Roland speaking now. "You wouldn't know how to come back here either, if you left. I'm sure you weren't paying attention to the street we're on, you guys wandered away from the center a little bit without realizing it, it happens to a lot of people. But you're not leaving; you must spend a little more time with us tonight, it's early still, you can tell us about the Madre Patria and maybe even insult us some more, so we can listen to your European accent."

Now I really wasn't happy.

"Look," I said, "I didn't insult you. It was Mike, he told me what to say to you and all I did was translate."

"Ah, you didn't do anything but translate," the fat one interrupted. "Too bad we don't know if that's true, we don't speak English. Whatever Elvis said we didn't understand, but you we understood, you speak very clearly, in a little bit of a rush like everyone else back in Spain, but we hear you loud and clear, and you can rest assured that we're listening. Him, no, your boss we couldn't understand, he was speaking English, right? We never learned it, we didn't get much of an education. Did you understand what the gringo said, Ricardo?" he asked Gilbert or César, who was, in fact, named Ricardo.

"No, I didn't understand either, Julito. But the gachupín yes; we all understood him very well, isn't that right, muchachos?"

Neither muchachos nor muchachas ever answered when he said things like this, they appeared to know that on such occasions their involvement was merely rhetorical.

I turned my head toward the door, the big bouncer was still there, almost as big as Hank; with a jerk of the chin he let me know he wanted me further back inside the dive. "Oh Elvis, this time you really have robbed me of my youth," I thought. They must have tried to come back inside when they saw I wasn't coming out but Pacheco wouldn't let them, maybe he even pulled his gun on them. But Hank had a gun, too, and in the street it was three against one, not counting Sherry, so why didn't they come back for me? I still hadn't lost all hope but I lost it a second later when I saw that the Villista with the butt of his pistol on display had left the table and was coming toward me, but only to go by and continue on out to the street, the bouncer let him pass, then closed the door again. He put a hand on my shoulder as he was opening it, a hand the weight of a steak, immobilizing me. Maybe the thug was going to help the rubberized Pacheco, maybe they weren't going to escort my group back to any hotel — there was no hotel, just the plane — but settle the score with the others just as they were going to with me, only outside the joint that belonged to them, dar el paseo that's called: going for a ride.

I didn't know which was better: if the others were being prevented from rescuing me or if they had left me in the lurch. Rescuing me. The only one who might have felt any obligation to do that was Mr. Presley, and even then: we'd only spent a few days together, I was an employee or peon, no more, and after all I spoke the local language and would know how to take care of myself; Hank didn't seem like a bad guy or a man to abandon anyone, but he was a capataz and his primary duty was to look out for Mr. Presley and bring him back safe and sound from that bad encounter, anything else was secondary, they could look for me later, when the King was far away and out of danger, what a disaster for so many people if anything should happen to him. But I wouldn't be disastrous for anyone. As for McGraw and the girl, no one could criticize McGraw for leaving me there until hell froze over if he wanted to, I hadn't lifted a finger for him when he was being strangled on a dance floor to the beat of a rumba. The music started up again, it had been interrupted by the altercation, though not by death which seemed to have arrived among us. I felt a shove on my back—that steak, so raw—and walked to Ricardo's table, he urged me to sit down, motioning with his hand toward the seat left empty by the Villista thug. It was a friendly gesture, he was wearing a deep red handkerchief around his neck, very neatly arranged, I only had to try to get them to forgive me for words that were not mine—though they'd been on my lips, or had become real only through my lips, I was the one who had divulged them or deciphered them—but that was incredible, how could they hold me guilty for something that didn't proceed from my head or my will or my spirit. But it had come from my tongue, my tongue had made it possible, from my tongue they had grasped what was happening, and if I hadn't translated, those men would have had no more than Presley's tone of voice to go on, and tones of voice have no meaning, even if they are imitated or represented or suggested. No one kills over a tone of voice. I was the messenger, the intermediary, the translator, the true deliverer of the news, I was the one they had understood, and maybe they didn't want to have serious problems with someone as important and famous as Mr. Presley, the FBI itself would have crossed the border to hunt them down if they had so much as scratched him, petty gangsters know above all whom they can tangle with and whom they can't, who can be taught a lesson and who can be left to bleed, just as capatazes and businessmen know, but not peons.

I spent that whole eternal night with them, the entire group, women and men, we went to a string of bars, we would all sit down around a table and watch some dances or a song or a striptease and then move on to the next place. I didn't know where I was, every time we went somewhere new we traveled in several cars, I barely knew the city, I watched the street signs go by, a few names stayed with me, and I haven't ever gone back to Mexico City, I never will go back, I know, though Ricardo must be nearing seventy by now and fat Julio has been dead for centuries. (The thugs won't have lasted, that type has a brief, sporadic life.) Doctor Lucio, Plaza Morelia, Doctor Lavista, those few names stuck in my head. They assigned me — or maybe it was his choice — to the company of the fat man for the duration of the evening's festivities, he was the one who chatted with me the most often, asking me where I was from and about Madrid, and I told him what my name was and what I was doing in America, about my life and my brief history which perhaps began then; maybe he needed to know who he was going to be killing later that night.

I remember he asked me, "Why the name Roy? That was what your boss called you, right? That's not one of our Spanish names."

"It's just a nickname they use, my name is Rogelio," I lied. I wasn't about to tell him my real name.

"Rogelio qué más."

"Rogelio Torres." But you almost never lie entirely, my full surname is Ruibérriz de Torres.

"I was in Madrid once, years ago, I stayed at the Hotel Castellana Hilton, it was pretty. At night it's fun, lots of people, lots of bullfighters. In the daytime I didn't like it, everything dirty and too many policemen in the streets, as if they were afraid of the citizens."

"It's the citizens that are afraid of them," I said. "That's why I left."

"Ah muchachos, es un rebelde."

I tried to be sparing in my information yet courteous in my conduct, he wasn't giving me much of a chance to show how nice I could be. I told an anecdote to see if they would think it was charming or funny, but they weren't inclined to enjoy my sense of humor. When someone has it in for you, there's nothing you can do, they'll never acknowledge any merit in you and would rather bite their cheeks and lips until they bleed than laugh at what you're saying (unless it's a woman, women laugh no matter what). And from time to time one or another of them would remember the reason for my presence there, recollecting it out loud to keep everyone simmering:

"Ay, why doesn't the muchacho like us," Ricardo would say suddenly, fixing his eyes on me. "I hope his wishes haven't come true during our absence and we don't find El Tato reduced to ashes when we go back. That would be most distressing."

Or Julio would say, "It's just that you had to go and choose such an ugly word, Rogelito revoltoso, why did you have to call me a maricona, you could have said I was a fairy. That would have hurt me less, now, you see how things are. Feelings are a great mystery."

I tried to argue each time they came at me with this: it wasn't me, I was only transmitting; and they were right, McGraw had asked for it and Mike hadn't been fair at all. But it was no use, they clung to the extravagant idea that I was the only one they had heard and understood, and what did they know about what the singer had said in English.

The women sometimes spoke to me, too, but they only wanted to know about Elvis. I stayed firm on that point and never wavered, that was his double and I'd hardly seen the real Elvis during the shoot, he was very inaccessible. In the third place we dropped into Pacheco reappeared, and seeing him really shook me up. He went over to Ricardo and whispered in his ear, his Indian eyes on me. Fat Julio pulled his chair over and lifted a hand to his ear in order to hear the report. Then Pacheco went off to dance, the man loved a dance floor. Ricardo and Julio said nothing, though I was looking at them with a questioning and undoubtedly anxious expression, or maybe that's why they didn't say anything, to worry me. Finally I worked up the nerve to ask: "Perdone, señor, do you know if my friends got back all right? The other gentleman was accompanying them, no?"

Ricardo blew cigarette smoke in my face and picked a shred of tobacco off his tongue. He took advantage of the occasion to smooth his moustache and answered, flexing his biceps (it was almost a tic), "We have no way of knowing. It looks like there's a storm brewing tonight, so God willing they'll crash."

He looked away deliberately and I didn't think it was advisable to insist; I'd understood him well enough. He could only be referring to the plane, so Pacheco must have taken them back to the airport on the outskirts of the city where we had landed, and now he had told Ricardo about it: no hotel, a small plane, otherwise there was no way Ricardo could have known, no one ever mentioned the airplane in El Tato and I hadn't mentioned it since. Now I really did feel lost, if Presley and the others had taken off for Acapulco I could say my last farewell. I had a feeling of being cut off, of abyss and abandonment and enormous distance or of a dropped curtain, my friends were no longer in the same territory. And what never occurred to me, neither then nor over the course of the five days that followed, was that the abyss would become or had already, immediately, become much larger and the territory much more remote, that they decamped immediately in light of what had happened, alarmed by McGraw and Sherry and Hank and convinced of the manifest unsafety of that country for Presley; nor that in Acapulco I would find, when I arrived bruised and battered at the end of those five days — five — only the second unit that even today the liner notes speak of, left there partly to shoot more stills and partly as a detachment in case I appeared; nor that after that night Presley never again set foot in Mexico but gave his entire performance as the trapeze artist Mike Windgren in a movie studio, my idea about the double was put to use; nor that I would not manage to be present for the climactic scene in which "Guadalajara" was sung, and which would, for that reason, become the most ludicrous display of the Spanish language ever heard on a record or seen on a screen, Presley sings all the lyrics of the entire song and you can't understand a thing he says, an inarticulate language: when they finished filming the scene everyone crowded around and slapped his back with insincere congratulations ("Mucho, Elvis"), they told me later; he thought his unintelligible pronunciation was perfect and no one ever informed him that he was mistaken, who would dare, Elvis was Elvis. I never investigated the question very thoroughly, but apparently it did happen the way I thought it had: they forced Mr. Presley to leave me stranded, first Pacheco with his threats and his pistol, then McGraw and Colonel Tom Parker and Wallis with their terrible panic. You don't like to think that your idol has let you down.

I was feeling hopelessly lost, I had to find some way to get out of there, I asked for permission to go to the men's room and they let me but the other bodyguard came along, the one with the pistol in his armpit, a slow-moving, heavyset guy who was always at my side, in the bars and also in the cars during the trips from one bar to the next. They had dragged me with them that whole night like a package they were guarding, without paying much attention to me, just part of the entourage, amusing themselves from time to time by scaring me, though they hadn't even made me their primary source of entertainment, they were a somewhat sluggish and not very imaginative group, the same guys must have been getting together almost every night for a long while and they were sick of it. I was a novelty, but the routine did not fail to swallow me up, as it must have swallowed up everything.

And in the fourth place, or was it the fifth (I started having trouble keeping track), they finally got tired of the whole thing and gave up on the evening.

We were a few kilometers outside the city, I didn't know if it was south or north, east or west. It was a place along a highway, a place of last resort, surrounded by open country, you recognize these places in any part of the world, people go only to drag out the night a little longer, halfheartedly and in seclusion. There were very few people there and even fewer a couple of minutes later, in fact we were on our own, two very tired girls, Pacheco, the heavyset bodyguard, Ricardo and Julio, the manager of the place and a waiter who was serving us, all the waiters seemed to be friends or even employees, maybe Ricardo was the owner of this place, too, or maybe his fat partner was. Ricardo had drunk a lot—who hadn't—and was dozing off a little, lolling onto the low-cut blouse of one of the women. They were criminals of little standing, whitewashed gangsters, their crimes were not organized.

"Why don't you get it over with now and we'll all go to sleep, ¿eh Julito?" Ricardo said with a yawn.

Get what over with, I thought, nothing had started. Maybe the fat one was going to give me some sort of punishment, or maybe they were going to leave me there. But they hadn't dragged me along with them the whole night for nothing. Or maybe the fat one was going to put me to death, the pessimistic thought always coexists with the optimistic, the daring idea with the fearful, and vice-versa, nothing goes alone and unmixed.

Fat Julio's white jacket was stained with sweat, he was sweating so profusely that it had soaked through his shirt and even his jacket, the combed-back hair looked grayer and had rebelled over the course of that eternal night, the long ends at the back of his neck had started to curl and were almost in little ringlets. His white skin was pale now, there was intense tedium in his eyes and there was bad nature, too. All at once he stood up in all his great height and said, "Está bien, as you wish." He put a hand on my shoulder (his was more like a fish, wet and stinking, it almost squelched when it made contact) and added, looking at me, "Anda, muchacho, come with me a while." And he pointed to a back door with a small window through which vegetation or foliage was visible, it seemed to open onto a little garden or an orchard.

"Where? Where do you want us to go?" I exclaimed in alarm, and my fear was obvious, I couldn't help it, I was suffering from nervous exhaustion, that was what they called that condition then, un agotamiento nervioso.

The fat man grabbed my arm and jerked me violently to my feet. He twisted it around and immobilized it behind my back. He was strong, but it cost him some effort to manage it, you can always tell.

"Out in back there, to have a little chat, you and I, about mariconas and other things before we all go to bed. You need to sleep, too; it has been a very long day while life, on the other hand, is short."

The start of that day was lost in remote time. That we had shot some scenes in Acapulco that morning, with Paul Lukas and Ursula Andress, seemed impossible. He had no idea how far away that was.

The others didn't move, not even to watch, it was the fat man's private business and there are no witnesses to these things. With his left hand he pushed me toward the back door, with the right he kept up the pressure on my arm, a swinging door that kept swinging, we came out into the open air, a storm was on the way that night and a hot wind had already sprung up and was shaking the bushes and, further back, the trees in a grove or thicket, or so it seemed to me when I stepped out onto the grass and felt the wind for an instant against my face, and then dry grass, without missing a beat the fat man had put me on the ground with a fist to the side, he wasn't going to waste any time fooling around. Then I felt his enormous weight straddling my back and then something around my neck, the belt or the handkerchief, it had to be the green handkerchief that had been forced to interrupt its work a few hours before and now he was knotting it around my throat this time, the package all tied up at last. It wasn't only his hand, his whole fat body stank of fish and the sweat was pouring off him, and now there was nothing, no music or rumba or trumpet, only the sound of the wind rising or maybe rushing away from the storm, and the squeaking hinge of the door we had come through, out onto the stage of my unforeseen death in a back yard on the outskirts of Mexico City, how could it be true, you wander into some dive and you don't imagine that here begins the end and that everything finishes obscurely and ridiculously under the pressure of a crumpled, greasy, filthy handkerchief that's been used a thousand times to mop the forehead, neck and temples of the person who is killing you, killing me, he is killing me, no one could have foreseen it this morning and everything ends in a second, one, two and three and four, no one intervenes and no one is even watching to see how I die this certain death that is befalling me, a fat man is killing me and I don't know who he is, only that his name is Julio and that he's Mexican and without knowing it he has been waiting twenty-two years for me, my life is short and is ending against the dry grass of a back yard on the outskirts of Mexico City, how can it be true, it can't be, and it isn't because all at once I saw myself with the handkerchief in my hand — the silk floating — and I ripped it in rage, and I had thrown off the fat man with the strength of my dark back and my desperate elbows that dug into his thighs as hard as they could, perhaps the fat man took too long tying up my throat and his strength deserted him, just as he took too long tying up McGraw in order to send him to hell, you need more than the first impulse to strangle someone, it has to be kept up for many more seconds, five and six and seven and eight and even more, still more, because each of those seconds is counted, and counts, and here I am still, and I'm breathing, one, two and three and four, and now I'm the one who grabs a pick and runs with it raised over my head to dig it into the chest of the fat man who has fallen and can't get up quickly enough, as if he were a beetle, the dark sweat stains tell me where to strike with the pick, there is flesh there and life there and I must finish both of them off. And I dig the pick in, one and two and three times, it makes a kind of squelch, kill him, I kill him, I am killing him, how can it be true, it is happening and it is irreversible and I see him, this fat man got up this morning and didn't even know who I was, he got up this morning and never imagined that he would never do it again because a pick is killing him that had been waiting, thrown down in a backyard, for a thousand years, a pick to split open the grassy soil and dig an improvised grave, a pick that may never have tasted blood before, the blood that still smells more like fish and is still wet and welling out and staining the wind that is rushing away from the storm.

The exhaustion ends then, as well, there's no longer

fatigue or haze and perhaps not even consciousness, or there is but without mastery or control or order, and as you spring into flight and begin to count and look back you think: "I have killed a man, I have killed a man and it's irreversible and I don't know who he was." That is unquestionably the verb tense you think of it in, you don't say to yourself "who he is" but inexplicably and already "who he was" and you don't wonder whether it was right or wrong or justified or if there was some other solution, you think only of the fact: I have killed a man and I don't know who he was, only that he was named Julio and they called him Julito and he was Mexican, and he was once in my native city staying in the Castellana Hilton and he had a green handkerchief, and that's all. And he knew nothing about me that morning, and he never learned my real name and I will never know anything more about him. I won't know about his childhood or what he was like then or if he ever went to high school as part of his scanty education which did not include the study of English, I'll never know who his mother is or whether she's alive and they'll bring her the news of the unexpected death of her fat Julio. And you think about this even though you don't want to because you have to escape and run now, no one knows what is it to be hunted down without having lived it and unless the pursuit was active and constant, carried out with deliberation and determination and dedication and never a break, with perseverance and fanaticism, as if the pursuers had nothing else to do in life but catch up with you and settle the score. No one knows what it is to be hunted down like that for five nights and five days, without having lived it. I was twenty-two years old and I will never go back to Mexico, though Ricardo must be nearing seventy now and the fat man has been dead for centuries, I saw him. Even today I stretch my hand out horizontally and look at it, and say to myself, "Five."

Yes, it was best not to think and to run, run without stopping for as long as I could hold out now that I no longer felt hazy or fatigued, all my senses wide awake as if I had just risen from a long sleep, and as I went deeper into the thicket and was lost from sight and the first rumblings of thunder began, I could distinctly make out, through the wind, the sound of the venomous footsteps setting off with all the urgency of hatred to destroy me, and Ricardo's voice shouting through the wind, "I want him now, I want him dead and I will not wait, bring me the son of a bitch's head, I want to see him flayed and his body smeared with tar and feathers, I want his carcass, skinned and butchered, and then he will be no one and this hatred that is exhausting me will end."

Javier Marías

"One of the writers who should get the Nobel Prize."
— Orhan Pamuk

"Sexy, contemplative, elusive, and addictive."
— *San Francisco Bay Guardian*

"The most subtle and gifted writer in contemporary Spanish
literature." — *The Boston Sunday Globe*

Javier Marías is widely considered Spain's greatest living
writer and has been translated into 38 languages. His nine
books with New Directions have been admired as "superb"
(*Review of Contemporary Fiction*), "fantastically original" (*Talk*),
"dazzling" (*The Times Literary Supplement*, London), and "bril-
liant" (*Virginia Quarterly Review*).

Translator of Javier Marías, Jorge Luis Borges, Felisberto Her-
nández, Flaubert, Rosario Castellanos, Blaise Cendrars, Marie
Darrieussecq, and José Marti, **Esther Allen** is a professor at
Baruch College (CUNY), and directs the work of the PEN
Translation Fund Award.